WiBBY THE WHALE

A STORY IN 3 PARTS

PART 1 - Playing PRETEND

PART 2 - The SUPER Gift

PART 3 - REAL Superpowers

While this story only takes about 10 minutes to read aloud, we know that the *most important part of <u>any</u> book for children is* the **conversation that happens during and after the story is told.**

By breaking the story up into a few parts, it gives the kids hearing the story a chance to pause and discuss as the story unfolds.

It also gives the grownups reading the story a chance to say, *"Let's save the next part for later"* when it's *really* time for bed. ☺

From the Author

The word 'acknowledgements' does not do justice to describe the support, the inspiration, and the loving patience of my family, friends, neighbors, readers, and colleagues over the years that this book was brought into existence.

The comments, questions, and suggestions from my wife, my children, my father, my siblings, my friends, the professional editing of Alexa Tewkesbury, and even the strangers who kindly read the words out loud so I could hear them in a different voice - they are ALL a part of this story about kindness.

And, a special tribute to Sr. Ann - a lifelong learner and teacher who started so many conversations with, "What are you reading?"
Even at 101 years old, I believe she knew how my heart would soar each time she would smile and ask me, "What are you writing?"

THIS BOOK IS DEDICATED TO

THE HELPERS

THE EVERYDAY, REAL HEROES
WHO STEP IN AND STEP UP
TO MAKE THINGS BETTER
JUST BECAUSE THEY CAN.

THIS BOOK BELONGS TO

_____

Part 1

Playing PRETEND

Our dear friend, Wibby
lives in the sea.

For a happy, young whale,
that's the <u>best</u> place to be!

Wibby likes swimming
and playing with friends,

but what she likes most
is playing PRETEND!!!

She pretends she is tiny
and can hide anywhere...

... or a super-strong giant
who can NEVER be scared!

She pretends she has legs
and can run on the ground,

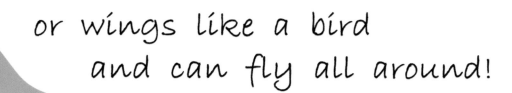

or wings like a bird
and can fly all around!

But, her <u>favorite</u> pretending
- her most favorite game -
she plays every day and
it's always the same.

With a wink of her eye and a
twitch of her tail, she becomes...

...SUPER
WIBBY!!!
THE SUPERHERO WHALE!

With an 'S' and a 'W'
on her cape and her chest,
everyone will know
by the way she is dressed
that this whale is special -
this whale is your friend.

This whale will stand by you
to the very, very end!

She'll have <u>real</u> superpowers
- always ready to help!
Stronger and faster
than just being herself!

And the whole world
will cheer for a superhero whale
who will fight for what's right
and never will fail!

Part 2

The SUPER Gift

Early one morning,
young Wibby received
a gift from her friends
too good to believe!

She opened the present
and gazed with wide eyes.
A superhero costume!
What a surprise !!!

The cape was bright yellow.
The suit, it was white.
The mask for her face?
It fit her just right!

The Super Wibby letters
on her cape and her chest
were just what she'd dreamed of!
How did they guess?

So, Wibby swam out
- not knowing where to -
just looking for trouble
the way superheroes do.

And while she was looking
for someone to help,
she heard a sea-turtle crying
on the beach by herself.

"I live in the sea and
lay eggs up on land,
but the wind and the waves
pulled them out of the sand."

"For my eggs to be safe,
they have to stay buried,
but there are too many eggs
for one turtle to carry!"

"But now that <u>you're</u> here
- a superhero whale -
things will turn out just fine!
There's no way you could fail!"

"Come up on the beach
and help gather my eggs!
We'll get this done fast
with your superhero legs!"

Wibby looked at the eggs
that were spread all around.
She looked at her fins...
They don't work on the ground.

The beach was so big,
it made Wibby feel small.
Without <u>real</u> superpowers,
she was no help at all...

"My powers aren't real.
It's a game that I play."

"I'm sorry," Wibby said
and swam slowly away...

She swam to the coral
where she hoped she could hide,
but a family of eels
rushed up to her side.

"It's a superhero whale!!!
Hooray!!! We are saved!"
And they cheered as they led her
to their "home-sweet-home" cave.

"We have this cool cave
where we sleep and we play.
A big rock at the front
kept the mean fish away."

"But the ocean was swirling.
The rock fell with a CRASH!
With the door gaping open,
they'll get in in a flash!"

Wibby looked up so sadly
at the wide-open door.
She looked down at the rock
on the deep ocean's floor.

The rock was so big
and she felt so small.
Without superpowers –
she was no help at all . . .

Wibby swam on
out past the reef.
Out where the water
is so dark and so deep.
She needed quiet time
to be all by herself...

when she heard
a small voice calling,
"HELP! Someone help!!"

She saw a little human
in a boat with no sail -
so <u>excited</u> to see a superhero whale!
"I was sailing along, fun as could be,
when the waves and the wind
pushed me far out to sea!"

"The wind was so strong,
it tore the sail from my boat.
Now I can't move at all.
I just sit here and float."

"But now that <u>you're</u> here
- a superhero whale -
things will turn out just fine!
There's no way you could fail!"

"With your great superpowers
you can fly me to shore.
I'll be safe on dry land
and not scared anymore!"

Wibby looked at the boat
with no sail on its mast.
She looked at the sea -
so wide and so vast.

The ocean's so big,
she felt smaller than small,
and with no superpowers,
she was no help at all.

Poor Wibby couldn't think of a thing she could say - just whispered, "I'm sorry" and swam... swam... swam...

swam away...

Part 3

REAL
Superpowers

When she finally got home
and saw all her friends,
Wibby didn't wear her costume -
didn't want to play pretend.

"Wibby, where is your outfit?!"
her friends they all asked.
"What happened to your super suit,
your cape, and your mask?"

She told them of the turtle,
the human, and the eels...

...having no real power -
how bad that made her feel.

"They were all so happy to see me and I really wanted to help."

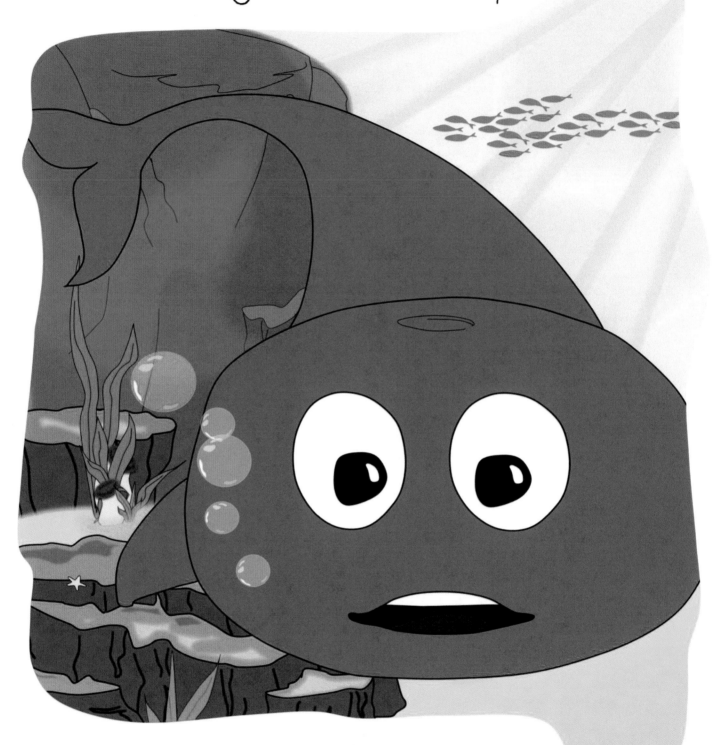

"But I'm not a real superhero. I can only be myself."

"And that's when I remembered how your present was so caring! You made me think of <u>real</u> superpowers - like BEING KIND and SHARING!"

"I felt so grateful for your kindness! I went back to them to see if I could be as kind to them as you had been to me! *Soooo...*"

"The turtle wished for a hero with superpower legs."

"But the cape was just the greatest thing for gathering her eggs!"

"The eels asked me
to lift the rock
off the ocean floor."

"But the mask covered up the hole
and made perfect eel-sized doors!"

"I'm so sorry I lost your present!
Will you still be my friends..."

"...even if I'm just a little whale
who loves to play pretend?"

"Wibby, don't you get it?
Your pretending all came true!
You helped everyone you met today
just by being <u>you</u>!"

"You don't have real superpowers,
but still you found a way."

"You were helpful, kind, and caring
and you really saved the day!"

"We all think that you are super!
We're so glad to be your friends!"

"You're our <u>hero</u>, Super Wibby!"

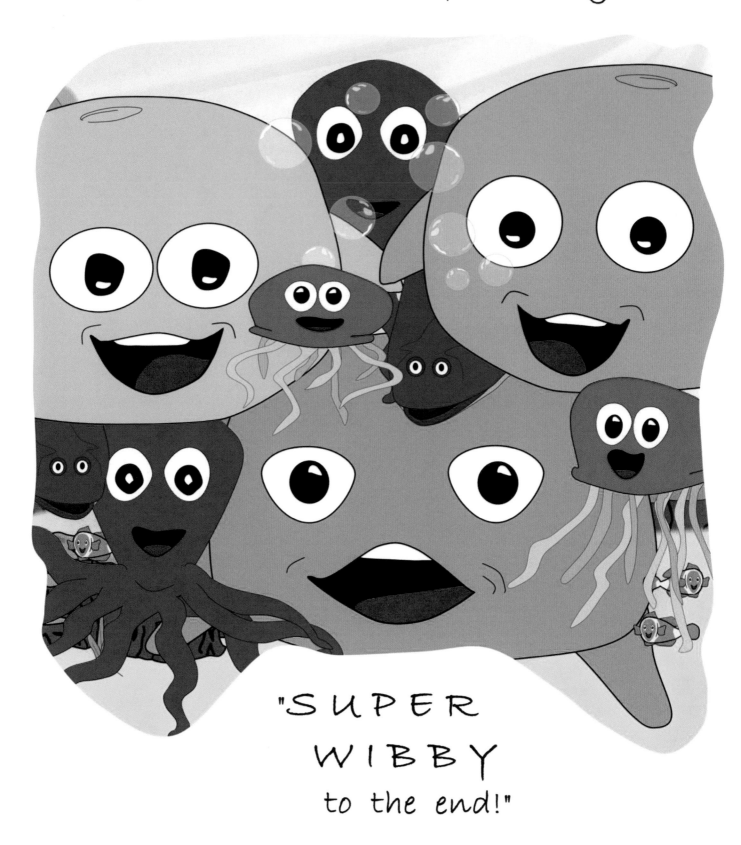

"S U P E R
W I B B Y
to the end!"

Other Finnegan McFinnegan books

An ugly duckling story where you don't have to be a swan to still be awesome

Because different people are supposed to be - you know - different

SCAN the code with your phone's camera to visit the Finnegan McFinnegan Author Page on Amazon

Or visit FinneganMcFinnegan.com

Made in the USA
Las Vegas, NV
10 December 2021